Miracles of
JESUS

Retold by Pamela Broughton and Diane Muldrow

Illustrated by Jerry Smath

🔖 A GOLDEN BOOK · NEW YORK

One day, after Jesus had begun to teach the gospel of God, He sent His disciples out to teach and heal people far and wide.

When the disciples returned, they wanted to tell Jesus what they had done while they were away. But the town was crowded and noisy.

Jesus said, "Let us go to a quiet place and rest awhile."

So Jesus and the disciples rowed across the Sea of Galilee to a quiet place.

The people saw Jesus leaving. They watched to see where He was heading. Then they took a shorter way to the quiet place.

When Jesus reached the other shore, people were already gathered there.

The people seemed like lost sheep to Jesus. He
knew that they needed Him to be their shepherd.
So He healed those who were sick . . .

. . . and He comforted those who were unhappy.

Then Jesus went up a mountain with His disciples. He looked down and saw that the crowd had grown even larger. There were about five thousand men, and many women and children.

It grew late. Jesus told His disciples, "Give the people something to eat."

The disciple Philip said, "Even two hundred silver coins would not be enough to buy food for all of them."

Jesus said, "How much food is here? Go and see."
The disciple Andrew answered, "There is a boy
with five loaves of barley bread and two small
fishes. But how can we feed so many people
with so little food?"

Jesus took the bread and looked up to Heaven. Then He blessed the loaves and broke them. He handed the pieces to His disciples to give to the people.

The fishes, too, were broken and given to the people. And, though it was only a little, and the crowd was huge, there was plenty for everyone after Jesus had blessed the food.

When the people had finished eating, Jesus told His disciples to gather up the leftover pieces of bread and fish.

They filled twelve big baskets with the pieces that were left after everyone had eaten.

The people wondered at the miracle Jesus had worked, feeding five thousand people with only five loaves of bread and two fishes.

At the end of the day, Jesus sent the people home.
He told His disciples to row back across the lake.
Jesus said He would come to them later.
  Then Jesus went up the mountain to pray.

That night, a strong wind began to blow. The disciples were in their boat in the middle of the lake. Jesus was alone on land.

Jesus saw that the disciples were in serious trouble, rowing hard and struggling against the wind and the waves.

In the middle of the night, Jesus went to the men, walking on top of the water.

The men were afraid. They thought Jesus was a ghost. But Jesus spoke to them at once.

"It's all right," He said. "I am here. Don't be afraid!"

Then Jesus climbed into the boat, and the wind stopped.

The disciples were astonished at what they had seen. "Truly, you are the Son of God," they said.

The next morning, Jesus and His disciples arrived
on the other side of the lake and got out of the boat.
The people standing there recognized Jesus at once.
They began carrying sick people to Him on mats.

From then on, in villages and in cities and out on
the farms, people laid the sick before Him.

And all who were touched by Jesus were healed.